Grolier Books

Produced by The Creative Spark
San Clemente, California

Illustrated by Yakovetic Productions

Printed in the United States of America.

ISBN 0-7172-8396-8

As Fun
As You Feel

It was another fun-filled day under the sea. Flounder, the Little Mermaid's friend, was showing off by doing loop-the-loops and swimming as fast as he could. Everyone was enjoying the show except Sandy, Flounder's twin sister. She felt left out and all alone.

"Nobody ever pays any attention to me," she pouted.

Just then Flounder landed in front of Sandy with a big SPLASH! A huge cloud of sand churned and billowed behind him, going right in Sandy's face. Some of the sand got caught in her throat and made her cough. Flounder didn't seem to care or even notice. He just swam away as fast as he could.

Ariel heard Sandy coughing and rushed to her side. "Are you all right?" Ariel asked. Sandy started to explain what had happened when Flounder interrupted her.

"And now, for my next trick, a triple back flip with a double dolphin twist," he announced in a loud voice.

"Wait a minute, Flounder," cried Ariel. "I think something's the matter with Sandy." Of course Sandy was perfectly all right. But for the first time that day she was the center of attention, and she liked it!

Sandy coughed a few more times, even though she didn't really have to, and then in a weak and pitiful voice said, "I don't feel very well, Ariel."

"Hmm," Ariel said as she felt Sandy's forehead, "it could be a case of the flatfish flu. I think we'd better get you in bed. I'm sorry, Flounder, but your show's over for today. Sandy needs her rest."

Ariel took Sandy to her own special grotto, and made her a little bed of kelp to rest on. "There now," Ariel said sweetly, "you just stay here until you feel better."

As soon as the Little Mermaid left, Sandy hopped out of bed. "Wow!" she cried. "Just look at all the wonderful things I can play with! And I have the whole place to myself!"

She took out some of Ariel's jewelry and tried it on in front of the mirror. She was so busy admiring herself in a pearl necklace that she didn't see Flounder peeking around the corner until it was too late.

"Hey!" Flounder cried. "You're not really sick at all!"

Sandy quickly jumped back into bed. "Yes, I am," she replied. "Ariel said so herself, and she knows more about it than you do."

"Oh, really?" Flounder said, getting angry. "Well, I think–"

"I think you shouldn't be bothering your sister," a deep voice called out from behind him. It was Sebastian the crab, and he was carrying a shell of saltwater taffy. "Here you are, my dear," he said as he handed Sandy the taffy. "Ariel told me you were sick. Maybe this will help you feel better."

Flounder swam off in a huff. He didn't stop until he got to the lagoon, where he saw his friends Scales the dragon and Scuttle the seagull. "Hi, everybody!" he called out. "Let's play hide-and-seek. What do you say?"

But Scales and Scuttle couldn't play with Flounder. They were too busy making a basket of pickles and seaberry muffins for Sebastian to take to Sandy. "I'm not sure about the muffins," Scuttle confided, "but pickles always make *me* feel better."

Now Flounder was really upset. He couldn't believe all the attention Sandy was getting, especially since she wasn't really sick.

When Flounder saw Ariel picking star-shaped flowers for Sandy, he couldn't keep quiet any longer. "It's not fair!" he whined. "Sandy's getting all the attention."

"Why, Flounder!" Ariel exclaimed. "I'm surprised at you! It's no fun being sick, you know."

"Well, Sandy sure seems to be enjoying it," replied Flounder. "Besides, she's not really sick. She's just faking."

"And you're just being jealous and silly," Ariel said. "Now if you'll excuse me, I have to take these flowers to Sandy."

When Ariel got back to her grotto, she found
Sandy happily sampling the presents from all
her friends. She didn't look very sick to
Ariel, and the Little Mermaid began to
think that maybe Flounder was right.

"Hold it right there!" Ariel said, scooping up the candy and muffins and pickles and putting them out of Sandy's reach. "You can't eat candy when you're sick! And pickles? Certainly not! You'll have to wait until you're better to eat these."

Then the Little Mermaid tucked Sandy back into bed and told her to get some rest. "I'll be by to check on you later," she said. "But right now I have to get everything ready for the picnic this afternoon. After that, we're going to watch the seahorse races, and then Scales is going to set off fireworks for us."

"Oh, great!" Sandy cried excitedly. "I love fireworks!"

"Yes, I know," replied Ariel. "It's too bad you're sick and won't be able to see them."

And so all Sandy could do was lie in her kelp bed and imagine all the fun everyone else was having.

The next morning, Flounder came by to tell Sandy all about the fun she had missed. "Oh, Flounder, I've been such a foolish fish!" Sandy moaned. "You were right. I wasn't really sick. I just did it for all the attention. I thought it would be fun having everyone fuss over me."

"You mean it wasn't fun?" her brother asked.

"It was at first," Sandy replied, "but then I found out that when you're sick, there are a lot of fun things you can't do. Like going on picnics and watching fireworks."

Flounder felt sorry for his sister. "I wish you had seen the fireworks. It would have been a lot more fun with you there."

"Really?" Sandy asked.

"Sure!" replied Flounder. "I like being with you."

"But I don't know how to do loop-the-loops and all that fancy stuff like you do," she told him sadly.

"Well, come on!" Flounder said. "I'll show you!"

A few days later, the Little Mermaid, Sebastian, Scuttle, and Scales laughed and clapped with delight as Flounder and Sandy put on the best show of swimming tricks ever. "I sure like all this attention, Flounder," Sandy said. "Thanks for helping me to be the star of the show, too!"